To Jonathan Nechemiah Cohen

SIMON & SCHUSTER BOOKS FOR YOUNG READERS
An imprint of Simon & Schuster Children's Publishing Division
1230 Avenue of the Americas, New York, New York 10020
Copyright © 1996 by Audrey Wood
All rights reserved including the right of reproduction in whole or in part in any form.
SIMON & SCHUSTER BOOKS FOR YOUNG READERS is a trademark of Simon & Schuster.
Book design by Paul Zakris
The text for this book is set in 19-point Frutiger Extra bold Condensed
The illustrations in this book were created with a Wacom Digitizing Pen,
primarily using Fractal Painter, assisted by Adobe Photoshop.
Printed and bound in the United States of America
10 9 8 7 6 5 4 3
LIBRARY OF CONGRESS CATALOGING-IN-PUBLICATION DATA
Wood, Audrey.
The red racer / by Audrey Wood. — 1st ed.
p.   cm.
Summary: Nona tries desperately to get rid of her junky old bike so that
she can get the Deluxe Red Racer which she sees in the store window.
ISBN 0-689-80553-5
[1. Bicycles and bicycling—Fiction.] I. Title.
PZ7.W846Re 1996
[E]—dc20 95-44061

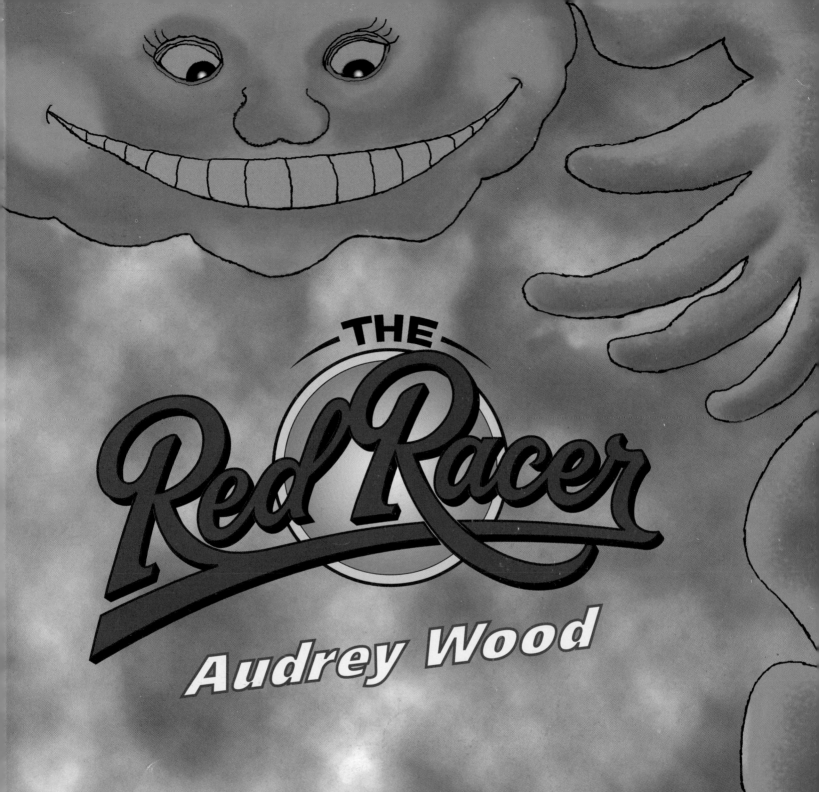

THE Red Racer

Audrey Wood

Simon & Schuster Books for Young Readers

Nona was pedaling to school on her old bicycle when the chain came off and the brakes jammed.
"LOOK OUT!" **Nona cried.**

She flew over the handlebars
and crashed to the ground
right in front of the
BRATS.

"There ought to be a law," Possum said. "No ugly bikes allowed in the neighborhood."

"Yeah," Weasel agreed. "It hurts my delicate eyeballs."

"Clunker, clunker, clunker," they teased,

"Nona's got a junker!"

Nona fixed her bike. She was already late for school when she glanced up at the window of the hardware store. There, glowing as if it were on fire, stood a

Deluxe Red Racer.

All during school that day, Nona could not

stop thinking about the Deluxe Red Racer.

When the last bell rang, she hurried home to tell her parents the wonderful news.

"It's the most beautiful bicycle in the whole world. We can buy it today!"

"You already have a bicycle. You don't need another one," her father said.

"A new bike costs a lot of money," her mother agreed.

Nona left the house and pedaled up the dirt road. She couldn't keep the Red Racer out of her mind.

That's when Nona had a wicked thought.
What if my old bicycle disappeared?
Then Mom and Dad would have to buy me the Red Racer.

Nona rolled her bicycle off a cliff and into the town dump.

Just then the doorbell rang.
"Nona," her mother said.
"Please thank Mrs. Org.
She found your bicycle at the
dump. You didn't lose it after all."
Nona thanked Mrs. Org,
then took her bike.

This time the wicked thought led
the way down to the pond.

What if someone stole my old clunker?
Nona wondered.

Nona rolled her bicycle to the end of the pier and pushed it off into the icy water below.

She looked around and spied her parents next to the pier. They were leaving the hardware store carrying large paper bags.

"Mom! Dad!" Nona cried.
"A Giant Pond Monster
stole my bike and took it to
his cave beneath the water!"

"Look, Nona!" her mother said.
"Mr. Carp saved your bicycle.
Isn't that wonderful!"

Nona wheeled her soggy bike away. She couldn't get the chain back on, the seat was twisted, and both tires had gone flat.

On the way home, she stopped to rest at the train station. The wicked thought was there . . . waiting for her.

Nona placed her bike on the railroad tracks.

"At five o'clock," she said, "the train will squish you flat!"

She hurried home to tell
her parents the bad news.

But when she
opened the door,
her mother and father shouted,

"Surprise!"

"We bought everything to make
your old bike look brand-new,"
her father said.
"We wanted to make you
happy," her mother said.

The clock struck five and the train whistied in the distance.
Nona knew she had made a terrible mistake.

Nona raced out the door and ran as fast as she could to the train station.

But she was too late.